The Burden of
Jonah ben Amittai

Other Books by Allan Brown

Figures of Earth

By Green Mountain

Locatives

This Stranger Wood

Winter Journey

The Almond Tree

The Burden of Jonah ben Amittai

ALLAN BROWN

Quarry Press

The publisher thanks The Canada Council and the Ontario Arts Council for assistance.

Several of these poems have appeared in different form in: *Nebula, Next Exit, Northward Journal, PRISM international, Quarry*; and in *Figures of Earth* and *Winter Journey*.

The author thanks the Ontario Arts Council for a number of grants received during the composition of this book.

Canadian Cataloguing in Publication Data

Brown, Allan, 1934-
      The Burden of Jonah ben Amittai
Poems.
ISBN 1-55082-022-2
      1. Jonah (Biblical prophet)—Poetry.
I. Title.
PS8553.R684B83 1991   C811'.54   C91-090408-1
PR9199.3.B76B83 1991

Cover art entitled "Nuclear Creature (Raven Series #24)," by Mary Weymark Goss, reproduced by permission of the artist.

Design by Keith Abraham. Type imaging by Queen's University Imagesetting Services. Printed and bound in Canada by Hignell Printing, Winnipeg, Manitoba.

Published by
Quarry Press Inc.,
P.O. Box 1061, Kingston,
Ontario K7L 4Y5
and P.O. Box 348, Clayton,
New York 13624.

Truth is a pathless land

JIDDU KRISHNAMURTI

for Pat

CONTENTS

Prelude:
The Burden
of Jonah ben Amittai

The indirections were simple
enough: Get there, dust off the doors,
say it and leave. But not that way,
not that way at all.

              At first
it seemed to be no more than a flicky grey daub
somewhere near the verges. Then it heaped, bruizing
till sunset and the panic held.

(It still does, usually,
about that time, a wait between
the darks.) But that was the first
and no remembering. Only
a kind of quick flutter, the sound
of that water-coming shape
again, moves, and a word
as small as stone.

              Images
of images? something out
of whack; the apple rouse
some fuller now, and patient
as who the new rain — unroof
my roof, Imagines, lower away.

Creaky it was, I'll tell you,
and damn' near scared the pants
off me — even took a new name,
but that didn't help — it takes
one to know one, I guess — and holed
down half a day there till seven
came eleven and they spooked me
into the nightly water clear
as time
       to moveless interfer-
ence of this telling
               foeffed me
to a pocket of hell's belly
crinkled *to taste the other fear*,
moulding, naked as leaves.

Neck-high and still
exhaling. A pestilence
of definitions stuffs my craw
each winterfull. The well
is very deep. Chunks become lost.
Nuzzle the fragments further
a bend or two; and yet
how slow the thunder and echo,
that dusty palm, returning. So.
A newer darkness and the rocks
are psalming, huge as loons. I'm oiled
through the grooves of it, breaking
downward. I split into my son.

The acted sea returns
             to test
each minute of my own contriving.
Merge the old letters are, done
and done again. Some lumps
on the bottom still and where
the seeded minutes one. 'Tis
enough, 'twill serve, if only
a near or throw away;
                    and is
no waiting other but is mine,
till red as ash the water healing
and to its own place restores.

Part One: Moss-Wind

The Lord sent out a great wind into the sea,
and there was a mighty tempest in the sea.
JONAH

(from the north the moss-wind blows)
MELVILLE, *PIERRE*

1

The plummet settled half a throw
and quietly, the cracks and code
together come.
                    Flutters the each
bland seed too long a waiting,
maybe, how to bulge the warm
and awful giving this; paused
delicate to enter, if
the blithe of me
a wobble out from such play
cautious to the season
weighing. Well. Taken the gate
re-sounds, and marrow is the way
to freeezing.

2

      Here the jantees
plump as any's kisses, scatter
poco a poco 'cross the thwack
of a green new'd dawning; and
neither closer nor beyond
the prophet's grave and under -
taking, gains of a saying
what these measures yet, into
lighten'd their westering further;
place and place the voyage
continues.

3

> The night wind rises.
> Is this a further way to live?
> My silver trims a warm breath
> now, the candles remaining,
> and they are still as any bone.
> A little loving would be
> easier to pause than this,
> I kinda think.
>   Shapes
> and the somewheres out
> of each expected turns
> 'em back to savour again.
> The growing's quirky. Even
> the least of patterns leaves
> me rubbled a softer tread.
> But wonder does as wonder is
> (the lighted minutes changing,
> obscure and most fitfully)
> and all these parted echoes hold.

4

Here is a green thing suddenly
(as near to the body
as shifty a truth can come)
leads thus its curious edge
outing his three-day wander
a bright of the waitful,
pale and necessary air.

And then the dove did, and
God-wording whole things never
a truth or not, indeed;
but climbed him back the how
each hair shaken, number'd, comes
a kind of satisfaction
only. Themes, if new-a-day
grown? the wayward pulse
continuing these minutes all,
and brach-me bellowing yet.

5

And then another. Nearly
did me too, the bugger.
                              Splits
the hollow each dark I do,
points me so to th' coasting plain.
The blue man in 's scraggy coat,
he gestured me. We heaped a bunch
for burning. (I didn't think
there would be time enough to pass
a chunk of him. I didn't think
I was his memory too.)

I'm getting thinner. Who's
for dinner? Mouse knows
the answer to that: go dance
on your toes.

                    This my centre,
still a much bendable thing:
but which next, Lord, my turning?
What taking through the neared dark
a patch and plug for Cerberus?
or how the way declines, or
where the voyage rarely.
                              One
and one my creaking birds
are subtle from their crannies,
bide for a learn-to they this come
a day more ready than ever
the pouch and pokey did; and shape
and not, my gullet bending
here an only spitful.

6

The fire is curious how
my glib and dusty rises — stuff
without stamen. I can do
another sorted thing — finds
me a bull for stoking, laying
greeney and grown to market
together; keep at it too;
not narry the first fizzle
in a chance maybe, but
I'm stealthy rounding with
my dexter sticks, pull 'em each
without a knuckle napping;
and here I'm laying again;
                      keep
certain at least the ashes
cleared away, ding out
the unflammable bits
and tender all t' others only
a little worse in the wet.

Spindle through, the downtime gnats
remember and a thing is done,
is cared and who in the catch
these wordings a-shuffled
be sorted yet; the nether turns,
the newly burns, and resheph
now I follow half-me upward;
bunching, touch'd, and droop again
skin-weary, in a wobble come
to briefly this held content.

7

In the deep nook, safely.

We're left to a cold bed,
you and I, some awkward floating
still before the silly dawn,
and least unprofitable
nears the grounding, mortal wind
a flat to say. There
is not a meeting to be
reckoned for us in or out
of taken's this time (*pro.*
ora)
     and I think the fire
is white now, dry and mooney
and very near; but not
him a new — do you see?
to whatsome entering; but
one in 's truckle bed alone
remembers and the rest
itself no longer limber
to.
    Nor tells the bone either,
of how those names were reckon'd,
each to come my knowing day
and day;
       or if she once
(who limned my gatherings)
in dipped the neither ashes
from this alien lake-to makes
a most of understanding.

8

Between their breathings
wait. It is the night wind
heard, loon-heavy, marks
another place than this, I think,
bare to the keepings of
Elijah's ghost, that raven man
deserted and repairing,
hopes him a little and then
a little more.
                    — Tried forty,
or fifty paces, was it?
careful in the mouth, and
almost made it back again;
too many stones, though; noisy.

What kind of a map is this?
The water's so deep my ankles
are getting rusty. A bit
of blood should see me
together. I'll nap when nearer
to the running place. This death
will fit quite nicely, I do
believe, and half a leg's better
than none. I'd shake a wing too,
if I had one.

           Anything
fills the come-to, with a bit
of practice: and do we ever
practice anything else?

9

But every new that solemn time
now's back-winding? something like,
it seems. A touch surprizes.
How very loose each parting is;
a dottle left burns right a way,
and spirits, they say, must live
in the places they lived before,
same streets and houses? I
gibber a bit now, learning
by rote each my degrees,
and verge me careful if count
through any the ways 'em how
the lean mouth deemed (is
here and clearly), holds yet
half the linden back; and slouch
me to the waiting mutt a jerk
and jiggle only.
              (Word-stuff
that, and drear the echoes,
gaming for once a candle
was, and who the worm to be.)

10

No bloody way. A softly word
will do. The piece of him.
Whether the big wind ruffles,
or who-we only that lonesome
whistle till all the crows
come home.
                    I act and patient me
a hunger more to tracing, as
my once the start in selva
to that certain seemed-of close,
the foggy shape, the shudder heard,
the elf and trickle beckoning
some further a day; and 'ware
the knowing obscurely that God
who is found in and through
every life is found in
and through every death also.

And if the voyage yarely ends?
Signs and seasons. A thin smoke clears.

Entr'acte

Deeper to 'm, was it?
that belly of a thought,
or something like,
              as if
a second in the sort
repeating Jonny's prayers
should enter now a tongue
to th' place where all our winds return.

The weather's falling, breaks
my lully to fill it
b' again; though wet's a way
of doing we scamper to,
and comes us shifty too much
to hold a sort of crisper world
for sorting, plummet-weary
but squawking still.

In a heaped house, how
the several air together
means this deeping who my yet
unanswerable day provide
whatever a one in 's world
to the next startle
reaching; will and known to here
the quick'd it chance again,
I think, that is and not the same.

(Or second's the place
to pause us yet? perhaps,
if through that sunlight cautiously
his webs endure.
              "The word is all
that is the case" and
heron be-done makes possible
the only seeing, and one
and one are the reaching wak'd
until however that day is come
the long recovering.)

                    In
a nick's the trick of that time
together till another fit or so
to pace the coughing wind;
nor yet my gathering
and burdy dead to fill
these placings and complete
the foxy paceless fall,
till memory wrinkles
the smear of Dathan
and Abiram seeded. Thick enough
are burdens (still 'em)
of again the mixing word,
or meeting paused a spite
of these —
                    a sorting thing
as yet the breaths remaining,
tighter, cloggy as yew lines
echo the spaceless dark'd.

And yet a pother done? Well
then, keep this further a close
it hovering brave into
each here and monotone,
or flaking teeth me
harrowed to such
that kenning.
           Slow 't now
in these casual breaks
of what the drying bread
sustained, another and
another saying? if
the river joy-us where
his pester'd mark endures
each day I borrow and
a guess to th' hair is who
enough will come.
            Were plumped
with burning yet, those seeds,
brittle to 's ghost; and yet
it done, winsome the earth
a thirty-full is new'd
and more; is get us known
then? yet and yet the Earth

Part Two: Intervals

On Hearing Vivaldi
largo e sostenuto

Contains 'em, and the fume,
the field-to, nude as now
rememberings dortour'd
are sunnerly bended,
drawing yet:
    A thing
is done, the boundaries
placed carefully
      till
gathered they all goings,
that truthing shout; or
come this to, seized, buxoms
a handed link is over
and again over the fall
is, even the fall to
one them the bend be done.

Three for Christopher Pratt

Barrie and Johnston Streets

The not very old men
in curling brown jackets,
with a three-day beard
(they share it between
them, and shave on Sundays)
peize delicately certain rolled
advertising statements onto
the sleek grey steps —
July in Kingston.

Girl With Sunflowers

No more than a year or two
into her puberty, mild
and slow, bending through the late
afternoon, the uncertain
strap marks on her shoulders pale
and augustbrown together;

and as the light changes,
caught, the slash of harder
than your white dress fabric
taut bikini briefs
flashing rectangular
image sharpen, glaze
to once the raise and spread
of your buttocks, weary
of time;

       haphazardly
moving, she enters a shape
of again the scentless
big flowers, casual,
releasing new minutes
into this warm, the deep air.

Eyes; The Dark

Startles they are
of now and quietly
the minutes of this night;

too awkward yet the touch
of them, perhaps, for mine
a measure to contain
this new and cheeky going
further a word
             who comes
and, parting, comes a bird's
wing of warning
to my lucid bones
only
     (cannot
the pale mouth)
             how
the ignorant flesh
deceiving here each gain
the troubled minutes met,
unpersons in this where
my silly name be done.

What The Bird Said

In primavera:
      green is the apple tree tho'
      notgreen I, having no
      alterable substance and
      rickety of mind
      so patient be to sign
      the falter into spring;

with no thing-
      memory to load
      the brittle catapult of truth,
      only a quivering
sustains, a wonder choose.

Like a whistle of stars it was
when Myrlin me worded there,
a 'mongst of silver in the grass.

In primavera is
      a kind and gained-of
      once upon the whole
      it, choice and choosing,
      delicate in this season, come
an only to be contented him,
and watch the strangely shadow pass.

A winter dew drop wets my root,
rippling into some second truth.

Five Sonnets

The Lake I

On a clear day, and when there is no wind,
the reflected image of the mountain
occupies the lake with great precision
of detail. One receives the impression,
indeed, of a distinction in colour
of rock from trees, even in the water.

Essenin spoke of it: *The golden grove,*
the ineluctable silence of things;
yet that itself isn't enough, necessary
but not sufficient, as the logicians
would put it; not even pars pro toto
in fact — both finally unknowable.

Those moving waters can't once be crossed, let
alone a second time, a second time.

The Lake II

Bits of the lake again. Twenty-five miles
almost, there and back, and nothing the same
either way. A looser recognition
now, sorts, separates the tangle, leaving
a set of startled illuminations.

Their faded sight be neither less nor more
unbearable than what that sweating rock,
the mountain dream, asserted was the form
the final cold would take. The cold is cruel
only to be kind.

                    He is careful and does
not move. Only his equal breaths betray
the casual identification
of map and mind. There is a sibilance
of aspen near the corners of this place.

Visitation

It is our unlikely interval.
Beyond that ending of each discovery
the hold remains, while *slowly, slowly she*
drew nigh, and slowly she drew nigh him. There
is only one ripening. Images
the images of their own death contain
to *hunt her with her ane white hounds* (this day),
with ruddy eye a-burning
                              … It is
that passing through defines them, how the edge
becomes again a kind of centre, and
the certain clue of each encounter known.

The intricate bough is forgotten in
this place; and always something else returns
to violate the limits of perception.

Hansel and Gretel
for Ken Stange

Everything different, everything the same.
They've both 'em come nearly so far as this
before, and manage to sign each turn with
a piece of "Nothing ventured, nothing gone."

They wonder the morning it why again
till, brittle as bread, they 're re-collected
and forgotten into a sorting way
together.
             After a while, though, it's not
as easy to cross that field any more
or less predictably; or wonder who
which sign was meant, the raven or the dove
reselving; till finally, unable
to see anything, they begin to see.

Poetry too is biodegradable.

Angel With Saxophone
for Allen Ginsberg

Tequila and salt come grey as a rain
hunting together, and no ending either
after the night forever seemed us, riding
and riding the flat and hungry dioxide
highways, away and away and only
a bitch of the memory still to come,
dreaming beyond our infinite shadows

(and somewhere maybe it happens again)

piece by piece through the breathing dirt, till one
in echoes of love for all the flower
we do, and our shaking crazy sticks sing
belly to belly in their gone places
ever and ever to point the verges
splinter-white, who in the bones of the sea.

Il Cardellino

A seemingly ownerless
kite heaping
across the sky, staggers
from one triangulation
to the next in slow layered
skeletons of thought;
                                    clouds'
shadows passing irregularly
over this field, like
Vivaldi's *Cardellino*
pairing and pairing images
in the thick afternoon;

until the brilling finch
releases into loosely
the song again, tones and
intervals traceless now,
nipping in and out
of their common chord,

pauses, inventing
simply its own freedom
perhaps, somewhere between
the chance for another
casual loss or recovery;

and the kite and the small
the bright bird in flicker
squawk and soar are how
again gathered into
their own unwondering
worded completion.

Entr'acte

*The colours of my luck
are changing, how
a touch is and the plea
to open such a knurly box
as this;*
              *stay the little till
our burly's most and done
to such a quiet death
you never would have known him.*

I'm truckle wet (d' ye hear)
a once before the having shows me
each this now for what a world
I'll used to be if bend me
another then, a bell or so
between the twitching waves.

(deep to the deep him calling,
swells limber a second day
and more till, filled, th' uncertain
spaces come a kind of heap
to pause us line against line
completed, who)
                          The places in-
differently urge 'em, deeped
that painting river and
the story twice a-told
contains yet how this going
is only the plain thing done,
the pieces to here a coign
and ending come; is hold,
enough.

Part Three: Aria Variata

And where is the place of understanding?
JOB

Lemma

A thing remains.
                        A same there was,
I used to think, could hold
each scatter 'ems on the water,
patient as who in th' breaking dawn,
to find what interpenetration
of founding both with capital;
or echo to my stones returning,
light between light till the wavy done.

Lemma: There is a knowing in
the least similitude can recognize
the pulse we are. And gaps 'em also
in merge of
th'eternal mix-through.

                        The sorting dust
remembers me; slyly advises, "Take
it one twitch at a time."

                        However wide
the net is cast, it cannot contain
the fisherman.

                "No string too small to save."

2

Breathe me a little, friend,
my upso wings are full of wind
today.
             I'm maybe ready
(yet I'd liefer not), so much
a dust I paced it softly
into that day of smaller things.

Yet's the place me waiting still,
and yet the trick it here
is plain to see how itchy-long
my twig will sag a further and
a further way, or
                              speckles
afloat, you say? and is
the certain place, or just behind
the sun's bulge early to th' cool
and watching air of each
our slow emerging, thingly known.

The morning's gone
without us, story, and both
without a word to bed.

Pastorale

There was a floated day:
                                How
we set out one morning,
climbed eagerly away
from the smaller,
younger growth, clear trails,
over the mists contracting
and firm line of the lakeshore;

was light yet a little
obscured in the loose bush
heavier graced, and wended
cautiously a wren's bone
further to th' dimness of
what occasion was before
the parted way, half
found, half made;
                                until
we broke into a soft,
the hidden meadow, as
the casual coming light
of thickly curled 'em yellows
and blaze of shelter here
absconded, waits.

                                (Is ever
a word of dear and doing to
the stranger curl of silence
in a place it cannot fill;
a piece of the long wind only;
this unconjurable grass.)

4

Even the first or second sight
deceive; freshness a crinkling sort
of image through the air
left over when the dancing's done.
Two's all a many in the ways
we are, are aches drawn thinner now
that sumnmer's over.
                            Too candid —
needs a shadowy bit or so
between the heron cautiously
a pace and then delimiting,
contentedly a fro and back
to some-a-thing known; the how
again my opening to him
shifty stumbled out of the dark
we doubled once upon a day.

The wavy's left, but that's an all.

Elegy
in mem. Robert Billings

The colours of the lake
are changing now, a rim of ice
persistent at the shallows;
wrist-thin, the casual trees
in *pie Jesu* scatter 'em
then another dying
than the pulse I followed;
                                        till
each my cones a warm taking
come new'd to next our meeting;
and broken here a bloody thing
to softly place and place
of my beginnings, a little
less than angels, patiently
explains, and done's the word.

6

The dust contains me. I wind
down slowly. Death's another.

The squeaky dance a moment
beckons fulsome to my seems,
the sweating ghost of each
renewal, patient as pain;
and is there still a centre
where deep'd that image lurks?
or something careful to be done?
Selah.
          The long bird urges
a scry of my girlsbody
looming cell by cell
until the counting's won.

(Explicatio: the question
it only each choice we are)

How a touch surprizes in
this yet a plumey thing,
and how each truth I wandered
imperceptive turns to gain
another rising place.

                    Grace
me, maker of eyes, lean to
a sweeter walking now.

(Explicatio: the question
still has its own things to do)

Raddle-me-roo, old feather,
a one to your gain; or
ever the birthing a kind
of all limits suddenly
known, are swift and true as
whatever parse of that vein-to
stirs in his raging daily
all the flowing Christs him burrowed
belly to belly in 's merge,
and dawn-he discloses
close of the painted dirt.

7

A ship there was, and it sailed
upon the sea, and the name
him through that cumbering in
the casual thick it till
a small place found.

A child there was, and he found
the little hole who emptied
veinly those chugging locks.
I surely a once am met
and entertained

the lithe and chosen shadows
'ware of, though is no return;
or how the splaying water
shrugs my long calling a word
or so again,

till unbelief flops almost
a gracefully doing now
in Shemsons of stories they,
brisk 's a rabble of jackals,
lewd as pickles;

are pluck'd the gates to gather
all a-boney th' known town, if
soul-thin only to advance
the something subtle river-
us a turning

maybe? Faith-man? Fatty's fool?
(Or only wonder's knowing
as the certain queries send,
descend, and back again as
open the frame

a pace or two returning
silently)
       Or both to reach
the soggy that our limits
be, the tendered here, that long
space a little

and a further on, to place
my ended ring in singles
the night; although yr prospect
yet, once and a time to hold.
Sparkles define.

Th' in-known sea a pace or two
ambiguous remains. They
are for portents and for signs,
the decent air dividing.
A thing is done.

Prelude and Nocturnal
for John Dowland

Still breezy, though today's too cold
for flies. Are none the melodies
a second's claim?
                 The sometime voice
of him familiar as the cool
of how that day renewing
taste and tinder, and all are
the choices shadowed. Pair'd to
a bone he, if the watch endures.
Count One. Away.

My broken dead them gathering
are minim'd here-to, where and found
each point of their recording; if
darker a mouth who gapes me now,
and all the ending is
remembered fitfully —
                 that wind
a loosened go-away into
the freely a place of 's any
again is sure.
            This delicate
now weighing of me depends
the once here etch'd him
a smear on the loose page,
till dims it and my chord is come.

             *

In equal night together
we another way or so
for getting, come and come.
Count. One. Or who
this saying shrieves to, if
a where the river joy-us
turning, shapes;
                        although
the place it knows uncalculated
yet,
      yet familiar enough
to heal each our courses
cell by cell explaining
how my token's only dead
to right and left of, covers
it slowly this accident
and pouch of bones.

Live and let die;
                        if
not, another will;
                        if
so, take Guido's hand
to whatever darkness
the single thing restores.

The Abominable Snowman

My spills are come a little closer now,
the lean of them, a thinner breath
than ever One-eye in 's roaring wak'd;
or how these scraps defining
the hunger of the bracken wind,
spooks him nightly
to the bare vein, whose cold
is cruel only to be kind.

> *(Maybe*
> *I've come too dexter in my late*
> *praeludiums; or maybe not.)*

Shifty the way until a found
and colder light who tells
the bird of my beginning; or
echo-the-heron patients me
another gain through each the intervals
of what that grey perceptive summer
in 's minute claims: the holy clamour
of my cedar walking, smudge
of blackberries.

　　　　　It's almost dark
enough to see.

　　　　　My five words are ready,
and to th' name him tendered now,
and each the helden thing reclaims.